Fire Truck!

by Ivan Ulz
Illustrated by Garrett Kaida

For all the children who have
found their voices through this song.

Ivan Ulz

To my loving family and inspiring friends.

Garrett Kaida

Words & Music Copyright © 1990 by Ivan Ulz
Illustrations Copyright © 2013 by Garrett Kaida

All rights reserved including the right of reproduction in whole or in part in any form.

Temple Street Press | PO Box 7071, Halcyon, CA 93421 | templestreetpress.com

Library of Congress Control Number: 2013946393
ISBN: 978-0-9896231-0-0

Fire Truck!   Fire Truck!

I want to ride on a Fire Truck!

Fire Truck!   Fire Truck!
I want to ride on a Fire Truck!

I want to sleep in the fire station.

Wake me up when the fire bell rings.

I'm going to slide down the pole . . .

Wheee!

Then I'm going to get into my

Fire Truck! Fire Truck!

I want to ride on a Fire Truck!

I have
a hook and ladder,
a hook and ladder,

I climb that ladder
and I hold on tight.

I'm going to get out the
hose and I'm going to

Shoot that water!

Shoot that water!

I'm going to shoot that water
from the hose on my . . .

Fire Truck!   Fire Truck!

I want to ride on a Fire Truck!

When that fire truck comes near, people put their hands right over their ears.

They do that because the noise is so loud from the siren on my . . .

Fire Truck!   Fire Truck!
I want to ride on a Fire Truck!

When that fire is all put out,
I'm going to jump into my
fire truck and turn it around.

I'm going to go back to the fire station.

I'm going to have a hot, hot bath, and

a hot, hot dinner, with hot, hot food,
like hot, hot chicken,
hot, hot macaroni and cheese,
hot, hot broccoli.

And for dessert,
I'm going to
have some cold,
cold ice cream.

Then I'm going to brush my teeth . . .

pull those covers up to my head,
and I'm going to dream about my . . .

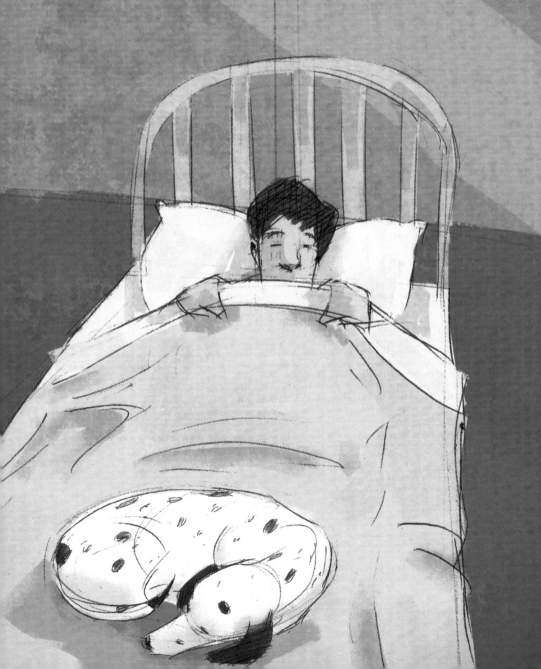

Fire Truck! Fire Truck!
I want to ride
on a Fire Truck!

Fire Truck! Fire Truck!
I want to ride
on a Fire Truck!

Fire Truck!

Fire Truck! Fire Truck!
I want to ride on a Fire Truck!

Fire Truck! Fire Truck!
I want to ride on a Fire Truck!

I want to sleep in the fire station.
Wake me up when the fire bell rings.

I'm going to put on my hat,
put on my coat, put on my boots,
I'm going to slide down the pole . . .
Wheee!

Then I'm going to get into my
Fire Truck! Fire Truck!
I want to ride on a Fire Truck!

I have a hook and ladder,
a hook and ladder,
I climb that ladder
and I hold on tight.

I'm going to get out the
hose and I'm going to
Shoot that water!
Shoot that water!

I'm going to shoot that water
from the hose on my
Fire Truck! Fire Truck!
I want to ride on a Fire Truck!

When that fire truck comes near,
people put their hands
right over their ears.

They do that because the noise is
so loud from the siren on my
Fire Truck! Fire Truck!
I want to ride on a Fire Truck!

When that fire is all put out,
I'm going to jump into my fire truck
and turn it around.

I'm going to go back to the fire station.
I'm going to have a hot, hot bath, and
a hot, hot dinner, with hot, hot food,
like hot, hot chicken,
hot, hot macaroni and cheese,
and hot, hot broccoli.
And for dessert I'm going
to have some cold, cold ice cream.

Then I'm going to brush my teeth,
jump into my bed,
pull those covers up to my head,
and I'm going to dream about my . . .

Fire Truck! Fire Truck!
I want to ride on a Fire Truck!

Fire Truck! Fire Truck!
I want to ride on a Fire Truck!

CPSIA information can be obtained
at www.ICGtesting.com
Printed in the USA
LVHW071926151118
597257LV00018B/313/P